Carly
the School
Fairy

Special thanks to Sarah Levison

Previously published as *Carly the Schoolfriend Fairy* by Orchard U.K. in 2013.

ISBN 978-0-545-70827-2

10 9 8 7 6 5 4 3 2 1   15 16 17 18 19/0

Printed in the U.S.A.   40

First printing September 2015

Carly the School Fairy

by Daisy Meadows

SCHOLASTIC INC.

The Fairyland
Palace

Tippington H

Science Museum

Tippington
Town

Kirsty's Hotel

Jack Frost's
Ice Castle

Rachel's House

Bedroom

Kitchen

School

My goblins are such a naughty bunch,
Why can't they just behave for once?
Hmm, I know what would be super cool . . .
I'll send the goblins to human school!

We'll steal Carly's magic objects,
To help the goblins learn new subjects.
My goblins will have so much to do,
And I'll get some precious time off, too!

**Find the hidden letters in the stars throughout
this book. Unscramble all 8 letters to spell a
special school word!**

The Spelling Bee

Contents

Competition Countdown

Rachel Walker walked over to the large doors of Tippington Town Hall and peered outside. Buses were pulling up and there were lots of people milling around. So far, there was no sign of the very special person she was looking for, her best friend, Kirsty Tate!

Rachel's school was taking part in an exciting competition. Four schools from different parts of the country were competing in two different events. A spelling bee was to be held today at Tippington Town Hall and a science contest was to take place at the Science Museum tomorrow. At the end of the week, there would be a dance at Rachel's school.

Rachel was part of the Tippington School spelling bee team, but the *most* exciting thing was that Kirsty's school, Wetherbury, was also taking part in the competition. Kirsty was a member of the science team and this meant that she was coming to Tippington!

"Rachel! Over here!" called Kirsty. Rachel turned around and there was

Kirsty! She was standing with three other children and a friendly-looking teacher.

"There you are! I was wondering when you'd get there!" said Rachel, running over to Kirsty and giving her a big hug.

Rachel and Kirsty were the very best of friends, and magical things happened whenever they were together. They had met on vacation at Rainspell Island, and since then had enjoyed lots of amazing adventures with the Rainbow Magic fairies. Jack Frost, an icy creature who also lived in Fairyland, was always causing trouble for the fairies. But the girls were always there to help outsmart him and his silly goblins!

"We came in through the side entrance," said Kirsty with a smile. "This is my teacher, Mrs. Richards, and this is the Wetherbury science team!"

Just then, an official-looking man in a nice suit appeared on the stairs leading up to the auditorium. "Attention, please, everyone! I am your spellmaster for

today's competition. Will the four teams taking part in the competition please make their way to the backstage area? Members of the audience should take their seats in the auditorium."

"*Oooh*, not long to go now!" Kirsty smiled, linking arms with Rachel. "Are you nervous?"

"A little bit," admitted Rachel. "But I've been practicing my spelling as much as I can! Come and say hello to my team, they're just over here."

"How does a spelling bee competition work?" asked Kirsty, once she'd been introduced to Adam, Amina, and Ellie, the rest of the Tippington School team.

Amina explained to Kirsty that the spelling bee was divided into two parts. "First, there's the Spelling Play-Off, where the teams take turns to spell a word," she said. "Then it's the Quickfire Challenge, when they have to spell as many words as they can in two minutes.

The team with the highest number of points wins!"

"Wow, it sounds very exciting!" said Kirsty with a big smile.

The four spelling bee teams started to make their way to the backstage area.

"I'll join you in a minute!" Rachel called to her team. "I'm just going to walk Kirsty to her seat."

The girls split off from the main group of students and teachers in the hall, and made their way toward a side entrance. As they walked along, something in one of the trophy cabinets caught Kirsty's eye. "Rachel, what *is* that?" she asked, stepping closer. "It's just the light shining on

the Tippington In Bloom cup, isn't it?" replied Rachel, still walking toward the auditorium.

"I think it's something even more special than that!" whispered Kirsty happily, tugging on Rachel's arm. What Rachel saw made her stop suddenly

because there, sitting on the edge of a
shiny trophy surrounded by a magical
glow, was a beautiful little fairy!

Rachel and Kirsty looked at each other
with excitement. Another fairy adventure
was starting!

Goblin Thieves

The tiny fairy flew toward the glass door of the cabinet. Rachel and Kirsty gasped, worried that she might fly into the glass, but at the last moment she magically appeared in front of the girls!

"Hello!" the fairy cried, flying a loop-the-loop in the air, "I'm Carly the School Fairy. It's *so* nice to meet you both at last!"

Carly had olive skin and dark hair with blunt bangs. Her eyes sparkled behind cool glasses. She wore a red dress with a bright-yellow scarf and a white top, and two-tone oxford shoes.

"It's lovely to meet you too, Carly." Kirsty smiled. "Quick, let's hide behind this cabinet before someone spots you!"

The girls and Carly moved behind the large cabinet.

"It's always nice to meet a new fairy friend!" said Rachel, giving the tiny fairy a careful hug. "But why are you here? Is everything OK in Fairyland?"

Carly sighed and her sparkly wings drooped. "Oh, dear. Something dreadful has happened, and you're really the only ones who can help me!"

Rachel and Kirsty exchanged a worried glance. "We'll do our very best to help," said Kirsty. "Please tell us what's gone wrong."

"I think it's easier if I show you," said Carly. She hovered in front of the glass door of the cabinet.

She waved her wand and the surface of the glass started to ripple. The girls knew that Carly was creating a Seeing Pool, a magical pool that could show events that had happened in Fairyland!

Carly turned around to face the girls. "You see, I have a *very* important job. My magic makes sure that everyone, both in Fairyland and in your world, enjoys school and learns a lot!"

Kirsty and Rachel smiled at Carly.

"That *is* such an important job!" agreed Rachel.

Carly nodded. "Everyone has to go to school—even fairy children. My magic objects help me look after the most essential areas of school time. My satchel makes sure that everyone loves words. It helps children read, write, and spell. My safety goggles make sure that science is lots of fun, and that experiments are safe. And my glitter ball makes sure that everyone enjoys music and special events, like dances!"

The girls looked at the rippling Seeing Pool, where pictures were starting to form. It was like looking at a magical TV! Rachel and Kirsty saw Carly in a classroom, polishing tiny wands. Next to the wands were three glittering objects— a little blue satchel, a pair of yellow safety goggles, and a super-shiny glitter ball.

A strange noise came from the scene. *SPLAT!* There it was again!

Carly flew into a classroom next door. The window was open and in the middle of the room were two giant green snowballs. A moldy leaf with a message was stuck on one of the snowballs.

In wobbly handwriting it read: *Ha-ha! We tricked you! Silly little fairy!*

"Oh, no!" exclaimed Rachel. "This looks like the work of the goblins!"

Carly nodded her head sadly. The Seeing Pool showed the poor little fairy fluttering quickly back to her classroom. But everything was in chaos!

The wands from the cabinet were scattered everywhere and desks were piled on top of each other. Worst of all, the three magic objects had disappeared!

Carly rushed over to the open window and saw four goblins just reaching the ground. One of them had the satchel clutched in his hand, another was wearing the goggles, and the glitter ball was being worn as a medallion by a third goblin.

"Stop, thieves!" cried Carly.

But the goblins made faces at her and ran away into the forest.

The Seeing Pool faded.

"I don't understand!" cried Kirsty with a frown. "What do the goblins want with your magic objects?"

"I don't know!" replied Carly, a little tear rolling down her cheek. "But

 now that they have them, school time everywhere will be in chaos! And it looks like Jack Frost and his

goblins are *here*, in Tippington, with my magic satchel!"

"What does that mean?" asked Rachel.

Carly took a shaky breath. "It means that the spelling bee will be ruined. The satchel looks after reading, writing, *and* spelling, and it helps people to concentrate. With the satchel in the hands of the goblins, the whole competition will be a total disaster!"

Spelling Silliness

An announcement came over the loudspeaker. "The spelling bee will begin in five minutes. All contestants please go to the stage."

"Oh!" cried Rachel. "I have to go!"

"Don't worry, Rachel," said Kirsty, with a determined look on her face. "Join your team. Carly and I will sit in the audience, and keep our eyes open for Jack Frost and his goblins."

"Great idea!" agreed Carly, fluttering into Kirsty's pocket. "Good luck, Rachel!"

Rachel headed to the stage. The teams were sitting behind desks on the stage. A large, heavy curtain shielded them from the audience. Rachel could tell immediately that something was wrong.

Instead of preparing for the competition, Adam was sighing loudly and tearing pages out of his notebook. Amina had her feet up on the desk and was playing her music out loud. Ellie was sitting on the desk, looking absolutely bored.

Rachel glanced around the stage to see if there was any sign of the blue satchel. She noticed that the other teams were also acting very strangely.

The students from Wetherbury were arguing, half of the team from St. Martin's was missing, and two of the students from the Manning school were asleep under their desk!

Just then, two judges came onto the stage: a woman with curly gray hair and a short man with a large beard. They looked flustered. "Where on earth can he *be*?" Rachel overheard the female judge saying.

"I have no idea," muttered the bearded judge. "We'll have to start without him. It's a good thing that we always have a copy of the questions, otherwise, we would have had to cancel the spelling competition."

"OK, everyone!" called the curly-haired

judge. "It's time to begin. The curtain is about to be pulled back. Everyone in their places, please!"

With a lot of grumbling the teams reluctantly sat behind their desks. A moment later the curtain was pulled back, revealing the audience.

"Welcome to Tippington Town Hall and to the school spelling bee!" said the bearded judge. "We will begin with the Spelling Play-Off. Each team will take turns spelling words from this list." He pulled a piece of paper out of his pocket, but Rachel could see that it was totally blank!

"Oh, dear!" mumbled the judge. "Never mind. I know that list like the back of my hand. St. Martin's, your word to spell is *zoo*."

From the audience, Kirsty and Carly could see the St. Martin's team looking very confused.

"Is it *Z-U-U-U*?" replied a small boy with thick wavy hair.

"Yes, that is correct. A hundred points to St. Martin's!" said the female judge. "Excellent spelling."

"Oh, no!" whispered Carly, shaking her head. "That *isn't* how you spell *zoo*! Because my magic satchel is missing, the teams have forgotten how to spell and the judges don't know either. This is a *disaster*!"

Back on the stage, it was Tippington School's turn. "Your word is very simple," said the judge. "It is *supercalifragilisticexpialidocious*."

"But that isn't a real word!" cried Rachel.

"No complaining." The judge frowned. "Your team has lost a thousand points. Wetherbury, you're next."

"That's so unfair!" cried Kirsty from the audience. "Come on, Carly. We have to do something. Let's head straight to the stage!"

Suddenly, they heard a commotion. Then a tall figure strode onto the stage.

"Here I am! King Spellmaster, ruler of all who spell and everyone else in the whole world!" cried the figure, sitting down on a large, ornate chair. He  was wearing a suit that was too short for him and a giant cloak, which looked like it had been made from one of the stage curtains. Enormous sunglasses covered most of his face.

As Kirsty and Carly got closer to the stage, Kirsty frowned. "That's funny. He looks different from earlier . . ."

Carly popped out of Kirsty's pocket for a closer look and squealed.

"That's because that *isn't* the spellmaster, it's Jack Frost!"

The Suspicious Spellmaster

Kirsty gasped. Carly was right—Jack
Frost was on the stage pretending to be
the spellmaster!

"We have to let Rachel know that
Jack Frost is here," she whispered to
Carly. "Let's creep up the side stairs
to the stage."

"I'll turn you into a fairy," suggested Carly. "We'll be much smaller and harder to spot." Kirsty glanced around to make sure that nobody was looking their way. Luckily the lights were low and the audience was chatting and not paying attention. Kirsty knew that their lack of concentration was a sign that the satchel wasn't with its rightful fairy owner. They hadn't even noticed that the "spellmaster" was on stage!

Carly waved her wand and Kirsty felt herself shrinking to the size of a butterfly, with gossamer wings on her back!

"I *love* being a
fairy!" Kirsty
whispered,
longing to soar
up into the air,
but knowing that
she had to stay out
of sight. The two fairies made their way
carefully toward the stage, fluttering a
few inches above the ground.

"ATTENTION!" Everyone on stage
jumped at the spellmaster's loud shout.
"I am already BORED of this silly
spelling bee. I have decided to make
things much more fun. Each team must
answer a question about *me*. After all,"
he smirked, "I am the spellmaster and
therefore the most important thing about
this competition. The team with the

best answer gets a million points. The question is: What is my favorite word? Get thinking!"

Jack Frost sat back on his throne, chuckling to himself.

The four spelling bee teams started chatting, but Rachel was staring at the spellmaster in shock. She had just realized it was Jack Frost!

"*Pssst!* Rachel, over here!" Glancing toward the wings of the stage, Rachel saw Kirsty and Carly behind the curtains. Both fairies were pointing at Jack Frost. Rachel nodded to show them that she knew who he really was. She had to find a way to join Kirsty and Carly so they could work out a plan!

She quickly decided what to do. If her team's answer made Jack Frost angry, he was bound to disqualify them! Even though Rachel wanted her school to do well in the spelling bee, the most important thing was to return Carly's satchel so that the competition would be fair.

"I think I know what the spellmaster's favorite word is," she said to her team, whispering the word into their ears.

"Fine." Ellie shrugged.

"Whatever!" muttered Adam.

Rachel sighed. She was really impatient to find Carly's satchel so her friends would return to normal!

"TIME IS UP!" shouted Jack Frost. "What is my favorite word? *You* may begin!" He stamped over to a girl with curly blonde hair and glasses from the Manning school.

"Um, we thought it might be *sunglasses*," stammered the girl. "Yours are very cool and you're wearing them indoors so you obviously like them."

"*Hmm,*" said Jack Frost, stroking his beard with his long, icy fingers. "That isn't my very favorite word but my sunglasses *do* make me look completely fabulous." He spun around and pointed at Rachel's team. "You, there! What do *you* think my favorite word is?"

Rachel ducked behind Amina. She didn't want Jack Frost to recognize her! She tried to make her voice a little deeper than usual.

"Well, sir, we thought it might be . . ." Rachel paused before saying loudly, "FAIRIES!"

Jack Frost stumbled back in shock, his blue face turning purple with anger. "WHAT! That is the most annoying word EVER! Your team is disqualified!"

Rachel and her team quickly left the stage. As they walked past Carly and Kirsty the two fairies fluttered behind Rachel's hair.

"Well done, Rachel, that was a really smart plan!" whispered Kirsty.

"Thanks, it was really scary though. Oh!" Rachel almost lost her balance as a gang of boys pushed past her and ran onto the stage.

"Aha, there you are!" Jack Frost said to the four boys. "Everyone, this is the replacement team from Icy Towers!"

The girls peered out at the stage from behind the curtain. They could hardly believe what they saw! Four goblins wearing baseball caps and odd pieces of school uniforms were standing in front of Jack Frost. One of them was clutching Carly's blue satchel!

Tricks and Treats

"Those horrible goblins!" cried Carly, shaking her tiny fist at the stage. "We have to do something quick!"

"Carly, why don't you make Kirsty human-size again?" said Rachel. "That way we'll be able to move around together more easily."

Carly waved her wand and transformed Kirsty into a girl again. The three friends peered at the stage.

Jack Frost was firing spelling challenges at the goblins.

"How do you spell the word *Tennessee*?" he asked.

"Easy-peasy!" squawked a goblin in an oversized school hat. "*T-E-N-N-E-S-S-E-E*."

"Excellent!" The female judge applauded. "Four hundred points to the Icy Towers team. How about *psychology*?"

"This is *soooo* simple!" scoffed a goblin wearing a tennis skirt.

He spelled the word in super-quick time.

"The satchel is turning the goblins into amazing spellers!" Rachel groaned.

Just then, one of the goblins correctly spelled the word *gnocchi*. When the goblins learned that *gnocchi* was a type of delicious Italian pasta, they started whining about how hungry they were.

"That's it!" declared Kirsty. "The way to get the satchel from the goblins is to offer them food in exchange. They're so greedy, I'm sure they'll fall for it!"

"Great idea, Kirsty!" Rachel cheered. "But where will we get the food? And how do we distract Jack Frost? I think he's way too smart to fall for that trick."

"I'll use my fairy magic!" cried Carly. "I'll create some delicious cakes. Then I'll make Jack Frost's beloved sunglasses fly away! He's bound to try to catch them and he won't notice what the goblins are up to."

"That's a terrific plan!" chorused the two girls.

Carly waved her wand and a cart of delicious-looking cakes appeared. Then the little fairy turned to the stage. She closed her eyes. A moment later, Jack Frost's sunglasses floated off his head!

"What's going on?!" he screeched, jumping up to grab the soaring glasses. He looked like a spidery-blue ballet dancer! Carly's magic made the glasses fly off the stage.

When Jack Frost ran into the audience after his sunglasses, the girls shouted, "Cakes! Cookies! Delicious treats! Come and get them!"

The goblins immediately ran to grab treats from the cart. But Rachel wagged her finger at them. "Wait a minute! You have to give *us* something before *you* can have the cakes," she said with a smile.

"*Booooooooooo!*" whined the goblins. "We don't have anything to give you!"

"Well . . ." said Kirsty, pretending to think. "How about that blue satchel?" She pointed at Carly's bag, which one of the goblins clutched in his green fingers.

"Jack Frost said we need to keep this," said the goblin in the tennis skirt, sulkily. "We need it to be good spellers."

"But you're AMAZING spellers!"

Rachel smiled sweetly. "I'm sure that silly satchel doesn't do much at all!"

"She's right," muttered one of the goblins. "We are VERY smart. Let's get rid of the bag. We deserve some treats!"

"Yay!" His friends cheered and the goblin threw the satchel at Kirsty. The greedy creatures  immediately stuffed all the treats into their mouths.

Kirsty handed the blue satchel to Carly. It shrank to fairy-size and started to glow magically.

"Thank you!"
Carly cried.
"I'm going to
take this back
to Fairyland at
once. But I'll
see you again
very soon!" After
blowing a kiss to

the girls, Carly disappeared in a sparkly
cloud.

There was a loud howl from the stage.

"You silly goblins!" shouted Jack Frost,
who had just discovered the satchel was
missing. "You're never going to win the
spelling bee now! We're heading back to
the Ice Castle. I want to make sure the
other fairy items are safe."

The girls heard the goblins and Jack

Frost trudge off the stage and out of the auditorium, squabbling loudly.

All of a sudden the real spellmaster appeared onstage, looking flustered.

"I'm so sorry about the delay," he told the teams and the audience. "I went into a closet to get a notebook and the door somehow got jammed behind me! Now we can start the spelling bee!"

Kirsty gave Rachel a big hug and headed into the audience. Everyone settled down quietly.

As the spellmaster asked the first question, Kirsty caught Rachel's eye and the two girls exchanged a secret smile. They knew that now, the best team would win fairly. But they still had to find two of Carly's magic objects, and more adventures to enjoy!

The Science Contest

Contents

Super Science Museum!

"Bye, Mrs. Walker, thanks for the ride!" said Kirsty, hugging Rachel's mom.

"See you later, Mom!" called Rachel, as Mrs. Walker got into her car and slowly drove off down the road, waving to the girls.

Kirsty Tate was visiting Tippington with her school. Her best friend, Rachel

Walker, lived in Tippington and both Kirsty and Rachel's schools were taking part in two exciting contests! Four schools were competing in a spelling bee and a science contest. When both events were over, a dance was to be held at Rachel's school.

Yesterday, the spelling bee had taken place at Tippington Town Hall. The competition had almost been a total disaster, thanks to Jack Frost and his goblins. The goblins had stolen Carly the School Fairy's three magic objects. Because the objects weren't with their fairy owner, nobody could concentrate or learn new things!

Thankfully, the girls had managed to outwit Jack Frost and return the magic satchel to Carly. The spelling bee eventually went ahead and was won by a school named St. Martin's, with Rachel's team a very close second! But there were still two magic objects to find: a pair of safety goggles that made all science experiments in school safe, fun, and successful, and a glitter ball that helped make dances and other events fun. Today the science contest was taking place at the Tippington Science Museum.

"It was so nice having breakfast with you this morning," said Kirsty. "And getting to play with your dog, Buttons!"

"It was so much fun." Rachel smiled

as the girls walked up the steps of the Science Museum. "It was very nice of your teacher, Mrs. Richards, to give you a ride from the hotel to our house so early this morning! Now, where are you meeting your science team?"

"There they are, by the museum map," replied Kirsty.

"Hello!" called a girl with long blonde hair.

"Hi, Sophia!" said Kirsty. "Hello, Ed and Paul. This is my friend, Rachel."

"Hi!" said Rachel, smiling at the others.

"Oh, there you are, Kirsty," said Mrs. Richards, Kirsty's teacher, joining the group. "I hope you had a good morning with Rachel's family. I have the schedule for today." Mrs. Richards waved a piece of paper in her hand. "Our science display is due to start in one hour. We're on stand *1D*. All the stands are to the side of the main hall between the Space and Flight zones. You have forty-five minutes to explore and then we'll meet by the stand at 9:45 A.M."

"Great!" cheered the whole Wetherbury team.

"Let me show you one of my favorite exhibits," said Rachel. "It's really cool!"

The girls and the rest of the team walked through the museum. There was a huge wheel in the center of the ground floor. Rachel explained that it was powered by steam, and normally turned around very quickly, but today it was strangely still.

In the Space zone there was an enormous rocket and lots of glowing stars hanging from the ceiling, but as they passed by, the glowing stars faded. The girls exchanged glances. They wondered if the exhibits weren't working properly because Carly's goggles were missing.

"We're going to take a closer look at the rocket," said Ed. "See you back at the stand later!"

"See you soon, we're just going over here," said Rachel, pointing to a room called *Light It Up!* that was all about electricity. In the center of the room, there were two bicycles connected by wires to a giant light bulb!

"This is *really* fun," said Rachel to Kirsty, jumping on a bike. "If we both pedal quickly, we'll generate enough electricity for the bulb to light up!"

"Cool!" cheered Kirsty, hopping on the other bike and starting to pedal.

The two girls pedaled as fast as they could, but nothing happened.

"That's really strange." Kirsty frowned.

Suddenly a glow started to come from the light bulb. But it looked like a very *magical* glow!

Kirsty stopped pedaling. Rachel slowed to a stop, too. Could it be Carly?

Cool Rain Forest!

The girls watched the glow becoming brighter and brighter until they had to close their eyes. They heard a *POP!* and a tiny voice said, "Good morning, girls!"

They opened their eyes and there, hovering in front of the bikes, was Carly the School Fairy!

"Hello, Carly," said Rachel.

"It was very smart of you to appear near the light bulb!"

Their fairy friend sighed. "Because my magic safety goggles are missing, you could have pedaled all day and you *still* wouldn't have made the bulb light up! Until I get my goggles back, no experiments will work. I'm afraid that also includes all the school science contest experiments."

Kirsty frowned. "We noticed that some of the other exhibits aren't working either. We *have* to find your goggles!"

"Yes," agreed Carly. "The good news is that my safety goggles are here, in the museum. The bad news is that they are being guarded by five goblins."

"The museum is big," said Rachel, thinking of all the different places where the goblins could hide. "Let's split up to look for the goggles. I know the museum really well so you two should stick together and I can get around quickly."

"Good plan." Kirsty nodded.

The three friends exchanged a quick hug and Carly fluttered into the top of Kirsty's backpack.

Kirsty hurried toward the Space section and Rachel headed into the Eco zone, which was at the back of the building.

The front part of the Eco zone was a mini rain forest, with lots of exotic plants, flowers, and butterflies. It was always really hot and humid in there. But as Rachel went into the section, she shivered. It was freezing cold! The exotic plants and flowers were drooping and the butterflies looked very sad. Two children, who were monitoring moisture in the air with a special machine, looked worried.

Rachel knew that the zone wasn't working properly because Carly's goggles were missing! She left the chilly rain forest and went into the Garden section.

As she went through the swinging doors, she heard a loud screech and a cry of "No!" coming from the back of the garden, near a big muddy flowerbed.

"Aha!" cried Rachel. "Goblins!" She crept over to the flowerbed. As she got closer, she could see several small people playing in the mud with spades, wearing overalls and caps. But, as one of the small figures turned around, Rachel saw that it was a muddy little boy, not a muddy green goblin!

As Rachel headed out of the Eco zone, a strange announcement came over the loudspeaker.

"HELLO! We are now doing *The Best Experiment Ever* with some cool chemicals, and—*OW!* Get your silly green hands off *my* special goggles!" There was the sound of squabbling and then a loud screech, followed by silence.

That must be the goblins! Rachel thought, and she started to run toward the stalls that had been set up for the school experiments in the main hall.

As Rachel ran into the hall, she almost bumped right into Kirsty. They heard the sound of clapping coming from a large group of children nearby, who were gathered in front of a display area. The girls quickly pushed their way to the front of the group. In the display area they saw four green goblins!

Snowy Scientists

Rachel and Kirsty watched as the goblins pranced around the display area, enjoying all the attention they were getting from the crowd of children.

The green goblins were wearing very long lab coats that they kept tripping over. Long gloves covered their hands and arms, and each goblin was wearing a pair of safety goggles.

"Carly!" whispered Rachel, peering into the top of Kirsty's bag. "They're *all* wearing safety goggles! Which ones are yours?"

Carly peeked out of the bag. "I don't think any of them are," she replied. "Mine are a gorgeous golden color. But if you help me out of here, I'll take a closer look."

Kirsty took off her backpack and put it on the floor. Rachel bent down and carefully lifted Carly out. The little fairy flew under Rachel's hair, and the three friends made their way to the front of the group.

74

In the display area one of the goblins was holding up a huge basin of water. Another goblin had a very large test tube clutched in both hands, full of white granules.

"We will now show you how to make snow!" shouted a bossy goblin with two warts on his nose. He was holding a clipboard. "Beautiful, fluffy snow! We're going to pour just a few granules into the water. Oh!"

The goblin with the test tube had emptied all of the white granules into the water. As the crowd watched, the water in the basin started to bubble and foam. The goblin holding the basin shrieked in terror and dropped it on the floor.

The warty goblin quickly slipped, grabbing hold of another goblin on his way down and making him fall over, too! Within seconds, all four goblins were on the floor, slipping and sliding on the gooey, sticky snow. The crowd thought that this was all part of the show. They applauded as the goblins squabbled and threw handfuls of gooey stuff at each other.

"Oh, dear." Kirsty sighed. "What a mess! Your magic safety goggles can't be here, Carly, or the experiment would have gone really well."

"You're right," said Carly, peeking out from behind Rachel's hair. "We'd better keep looking for them."

"Let's look in the Flight zone next," Rachel suggested.

As the three friends made their way through the Science Museum, they could see all sorts of things going wrong.

In the Manning School's display area, the students were trying to demonstrate how magnets worked, but the magnets kept falling to the ground!

Rachel waved at her friends from the Tippington School science team. They all looked very sad. She could see that the balloons they were trying to blow up for their balloon rocket experiment had big holes in them, and that the nose cone had fallen off the rocket.

"Look out!" cried a voice suddenly as the girls walked into the Flight zone. A model airplane swooped down close to the girls' heads, forcing them to duck!

"Sorry!" called a young boy, running past them with the plane controls in his hand. "The plane seems to have a mind of its own today!"

"It must be hard to control because your goggles are missing," said Kirsty, turning to look at Carly. But both

Rachel and Carly were staring up at the ceiling of the Science Museum. Kirsty followed their gaze. There, dangling from the window of a *real* fighter plane hung from the ceiling, were Carly's magic goggles!

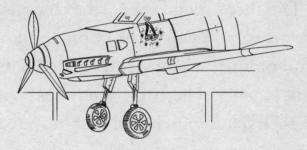

Flying High

"Hooray! We've found the goggles!"
cheered Kirsty. She looked up at the
plane again. It was a long way up. "But
how do we get them back?"

Carly, who was fluttering up and down
in excitement, paused. "Maybe I could
fly up," she said thoughtfully. "But I'm
worried about being hit by one of those
big model planes."

"Why don't you turn us into fairies too?" Rachel suggested. "That way we can work as a fairy team!"

"That's a great idea," agreed Carly.

The three friends headed to a quiet corner. Carly waved her wand and a trail of fairy sparkles surrounded Kirsty and Rachel. The two friends held hands as they felt themselves shrinking to fairy-size. It was the best feeling in the world!

The three fairies
looked up at
the goggles.

"We're going
to have to be
very careful up
there," said Rachel
thoughtfully. "There
are lots of airplanes
flying around."

"I have an idea!" said Kirsty, as she
looked at the small planes flying through
the air. "Why don't we use a model
plane to reach the goggles? We're just
the right size to fit in one!"

"Great plan, Kirsty!" said Carly.
"I'll use my fairy magic to fly the plane.
We can go right past the goggles and
grab them!"

The three friends carefully made their
way to the model planes. There were
quite a few people around, but luckily,
they were very busy trying to control
the low-flying planes! The fairies quickly
hopped into a dark blue model plane
and Carly waved her wand. The
propeller started to turn and seconds later
they were off!

In no time at all, they were up in the air next to the fighter plane. But as they swooped closer to the window, they got a shock: there was a goblin in the cockpit!

"Oh, no!" cried Kirsty. "That goblin is guarding your goggles, Carly. If we get close enough to grab the goggles, he'll be able to grab *us*!"

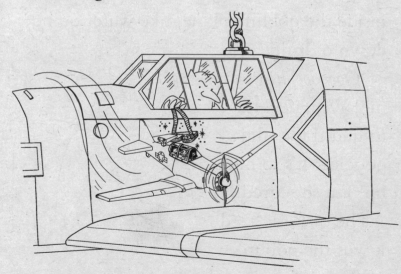

Carly landed the model plane on top of the real plane and the three friends carefully climbed out. As they peered over the side, they gulped. They were a long way up. Rachel and Kirsty were very glad they had wings!

"What's that strange noise?" asked Rachel. The friends listened. There was a glugging, squelching noise coming from inside the goblin's plane, like water going down a drain.

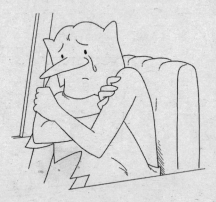

"*Ooooooooh!* Poor me! Why do *I* have to guard the silly goggles? It's so high up! I'm so scared!"

The girls realized it was the goblin, sniffling and crying!

"I wonder how we can trick the goblin into giving us the goggles," said Kirsty thoughtfully.

"I know!" squealed Carly. "If I use my magic to make him small and give him wings, he'll be able to join his friends down on the ground and *we* can get the magic goggles!"

"Let's try it!" said Kirsty, and the friends fluttered over to the plane's window. It was time to trick the goblin!

A Plane and a Plan!

The goblin spotted the three friends and opened the window.

"What do *you* want?" He scowled.

"*Oooooh*, we're having a great time flying around!" Rachel said, doing a figure eight in the air. "We can go wherever we want!"

"Don't rub it in." The goblin sniffed.

"Jack Frost used his magic to put me up here so I could look after the silly goggles. But I've been stuck here in this plane forever. I'm scared, cold, and hungry!"

"Poor you," said Kirsty, "and all your friends are having so much fun down on the ground!"

"I'd do anything to get down," said the goblin wistfully, peering out of the plane window at the ground far below.

"Well," said Carly, pretending to think. "You've done such a good job of looking after the goggles that I'm sure Jack Frost would want you to go and join your  friends. After all, the goggles can't go anywhere! I'm too little to carry them to the ground. Why don't I help you get down and *we'll* look after the goggles up here?"

Kirsty and Rachel gave each other a small smile. Clever Carly was telling the truth! She couldn't carry the goggles down to the ground by herself when they

were big, but with the goblin out of the way she could use her magic to shrink them to fairy-size!

"*Hmmm,*" said the goblin, thinking hard. "I guess so. After all, you pesky fairies are the size of fleas so what harm could you do?"

Carly frowned. What a rude goblin!

"I'm going to make you small and give you wings," she said. "The magic won't last for very long so you have to fly straight down to the ground."

Carly waved her wand and the goblin shrank to fairy-size, complete with leathery green wings! He looked very

scared. Kirsty felt
sorry for him so
she took his
hand and flew
with him down
to the ground,
being careful to
stay close to the
wall out of sight *and*

out of the way of the model planes.

They landed just behind the glider
and immediately the goblin became his
normal size again. He was so happy
to have his feet on the ground that he
immediately ran off to find his friends.
It looked like he had forgotten all about
Carly's goggles!

A moment later, the blue model plane
landed and Rachel and Carly climbed

out. The goggles were now fairy-size!
Carly turned Kirsty and Rachel back to
their normal size.

"Thank you,
girls!" She smiled.
"It's time for
me to return
the magic
goggles to
Fairyland
and it's time
for your science
presentation, Kirsty!"
She blew a kiss to the girls and
disappeared in a glittering cloud.

The two friends raced back to the main
hall. As they ran through the different
zones, they could see that things were
back to normal again: the model planes

were under control, the steam wheel was turning quickly, and the space rocket was surrounded by hundreds of glowing stars. There was no sign of the goblins. The girls thought they must have gone back to the Ice Castle when they realized they had lost the goggles.

Kirsty reached stand *1D* and quickly pulled on her lab coat and safety goggles.

Rachel stood at the front of the crowd to watch the Wetherbury experiment.

It involved making multicolored bubbles in lots of different sizes. The bubbles floated and flew around the area like a magic moving rainbow!

Everything went perfectly and the audience cheered as Kirsty's school was awarded first place.

Rachel was pleased to see that the other schools, whose experiments went badly when Carly's goggles were with the goblin, had the chance to do them again and they all worked really well.

"What an exciting day!" said Kirsty a little later, as the two friends sat in the Science Museum's café, enjoying frothy hot chocolate with marshmallows.

"It was," agreed Rachel. "And the adventure isn't over yet. Tomorrow is the school dance, and we still have one more magic object to find!"

The Dazzling Dance

Contents

Dance Countdown

"*Phew!* There's so much to do," said Rachel, looking at the huge pile of decorations in front of her.

"I know," replied Kirsty, untangling a long string of sparkly crepe paper. "But the hall will look great when it's decorated!"

The two friends were at Tippington
School, starting to get things ready
for the dance that evening. They had
spent the last few days together, as their
schools and two others were taking part
in a competition, which had included a
spelling bee and a science contest. Both
events had almost been a disaster because
Jack Frost and his goblins had stolen
Carly the School Fairy's magic objects!
But the girls and their fairy friend had
outwitted them.

Now there was just one of Carly's
objects left to find—the magic glitter
ball. This made sure that all special
school events, such as field days and
dances, went well.

"I wonder where everyone else is?"
asked Rachel, looking at the clock on

the hall wall. "We said we'd meet here at ten o'clock."

"How many of you are there on the organizing committee?" asked Kirsty while searching in the bag of decorations. *"Oooh!"* she cried, snatching her hand away from the bag.

"Are you all right?" asked Rachel.

"Something tickled my hand," said Kirsty, looking surprised.

All of a sudden
the crepe paper
flew up into
the air. One
of the
triangles of
material
unfurled
and a
tiny fairy
shot out!

"Hello,
girls!" called
Carly, shaking her wings and
smoothing her dark hair. "I'm sorry, I
didn't mean to scare you by appearing
so suddenly."

"Hi, Carly," said Rachel. "It's
wonderful to see you again!"

"Thank you so much for helping me get my satchel and goggles back," said Carly, landing on Rachel's shoulder. "But I'm afraid that your dance tonight will go horribly wrong if we don't find my glitter ball soon!"

Suddenly, the friends heard an enormous crash, followed by loud howls. The noise startled Carly so much that she shot back up into the air like a tiny firework!

"What is that racket?" cried Kirsty, covering her ears with her hands.

"I think it's coming from one of the music rooms," said Rachel. "Let's investigate!"

The three friends made their way toward the music department. As they approached the door to the practice room, the noise stopped, and instead, the girls heard familiar voices . . . goblin voices!

Kirsty, Rachel, and Carly peered into the room. The five missing members

of the organizing committee were
sitting down on the floor, paying close
attention to three goblins. The goblins
were dressed in oversized T-shirts, baggy
pants, and baseball hats. They were
standing by a drum kit, and each one
was holding a microphone.

"Well, that explains the noise," muttered Carly. "But I can't see my glitter ball."

"Let's listen in to see if they give us any clues," said Kirsty.

"You see," they heard one of the goblins say, "as we've just demonstrated, we are *fantastic* musicians. We're going to play at your dance tonight!"

"Awesome!" said Phil, who was in

Rachel's class. "It's going to be great when you start at Tippington School!"

"What?" spluttered Rachel, as Kirsty quickly closed the door. "Why are the goblins coming to my school? And why don't the others notice how strange they look? Something funny is going on."

"Yes." Carly frowned. "My glitter ball must be nearby and its magical powers are making your friends think the goblins are just cool, funny kids. But I don't know why the goblins think they'll be coming to school here.

I'm going to go to Fairyland and see what I can find out. I'll be back soon!" Carly blew a kiss to the girls and disappeared in a whirl of sparkles.

The door of the music room opened, and the boys and girls came out. "Oh, hello!" said one of the girls. "Sorry we're late. We're ready to help out now."

Kirsty and Rachel exchanged a glance. They really wanted to stay close to the goblins, but they had to get things ready for the dance that evening.

"OK." Rachel smiled. "Let's get decorating." Hunting for the glitter ball would have to wait until later!

Goblin Students

"Your dress is so pretty," said Rachel, smiling at Kirsty as she twirled in front of the mirror. "I love the sequins on it!"

"Thanks," said Kirsty. "Yours is beautiful, too. Blue really suits you!"

The two friends were at Rachel's house, getting ready for the school dance. They had spent most of the

day at Tippington School, decorating
the hall and getting all the tables set
up for the party food and drink. It had
been hard work. With Carly's glitter
ball missing, lots of the decorations
kept falling down or were mysteriously
broken. The girls and the rest of the
committee had done their best, but they
knew they had to get the glitter ball back
to Carly as soon as possible!

"I wonder what those sneaky goblins

were up to today,"
said Rachel,
fastening her
hair with a
glittery clip. "It
seems strange
that we didn't see
them all afternoon."

"We should head back to school soon," said Kirsty. "If we get there before everyone else, hopefully we'll find the goblins *and* the glitter ball!"

The girls ran down to the kitchen to see what time they could get a ride to school. Both of Rachel's parents were making party food for the school dance. As Rachel pushed open the kitchen door, a cloud of smoke drifted out.

"Is everything OK?" Kirsty coughed. "What happened?"

"Oh, dear, things aren't going well at all with the dance food!" said Mr. Walker, wiping a smudge of flour from his nose. "Normally my cheese straws are delicious but these are terrible."

"My brownies aren't very tasty either." Mrs. Walker groaned. "And they seem to have a strange green tinge. Girls, do you want a ride to school soon? I think I'll drop you off and then

come back here to try to figure out
the food."

Kirsty suddenly
spotted a flurry of
sparkles in the
corner of the
kitchen. There
was Carly,
hiding behind a
box of flour! She
nudged Rachel,

who moved closer to Carly so the pretty
little fairy could flutter behind her hair.

"Yes, please, Mom," Rachel said.
"Can we leave in about five minutes?
We just need to get a few more things
together for the dance."

The girls quickly ran back up the stairs
to Rachel's room.

"Hi, again, girls," said Carly. "I've had a *very* busy day in Fairyland, trying to find out what's going on and why Jack Frost wanted my magic objects. I'll create a Seeing Pool so I can show you what's been happening."

The little fairy fluttered up to Rachel's mirror and waved her wand. A rippling picture emerged.

The scene showed Jack Frost and his goblins in a classroom. Jack Frost seemed to be trying to teach the goblins math. But the goblins used the pen and paper he had given them to

draw silly pictures of each other and
to make paper airplanes. The scene faded.

Then, Rachel and Kirsty saw Jack
Frost peeking into Carly's classroom in
Fairyland. Sitting at their desks were
lots of well-behaved fairy children, all
listening carefully to Carly's lesson.

"AHA! School is what my silly goblins need," cried Jack Frost. "I'll send them to a *real* school in the human world. That will teach the goblins to respect my authority and listen to ME! We'll steal the objects that belong to that silly fairy, so my goblins get a head start at school. *Hee hee!*"

With the sound of Jack Frost's icy chuckle ringing in everyone's ears, the Seeing Pool faded. Carly turned to the girls, her pretty face serious. "You

see, Jack Frost stole my magic objects to control the goblins. He thinks that sending them to school in the human world will make them better behaved."

The girls nodded at Carly. This was terrible news!

Surprising Sounds

Rachel and Kirsty looked at each other in shock. "But . . . but the goblins can't go to school in our world," said Kirsty. "People will soon notice that they are anything but human!"

"You're right," said Rachel. "We must get the glitter ball back and make the goblins go home to the Ice Castle before they cause any more trouble."

The girls put their shoes and coats on, and waited in the hall for Mrs. Walker. They felt a little sorry for Rachel's mom and dad—as long as the glitter ball was missing, all the food her parents made for the dance would taste awful!

Just a few minutes later, Kirsty and Rachel arrived at Tippington School, with Carly hiding in Rachel's bag. They

made their way
to the school
gym, looking
in each
room to
see if they
could spot
any goblin
activity,
but all was
quiet. The dance
wasn't due to start
for another half an hour and there was
nobody around.

The gym should have been beautiful
after all the decorating, but instead it
looked messy. The crepe paper had fallen
down and the helium balloons were on
the floor.

"Let's see if the colored lights work,"
said Kirsty, flicking the light switch.
The lights came on and flashed prettily,
sparkling against the disco balls that
were hanging in front of the stage. Kirsty
and Rachel smiled at each other happily.
But then, one by one, the lights went out
until just the green light remained on,
casting a spooky green glow around
the room.

Suddenly, the girls heard a familiar icy voice coming from the side of the stage.

"Get out of my way. *I'm* the lead singer in this group and *I* need to check my vocals!" It was Jack Frost!

The three friends quickly ducked under the party food table. Then they peeked out and saw three goblins following Jack Frost. Each goblin was wearing a tight white jumpsuit, decorated with silver lightning bolts. Two goblins carried guitars and the third headed to the drum set already on stage.

Jack Frost was wearing a baggy white and silver jumpsuit with a pair of huge silver high-top sneakers that made him even taller than usual. Perched on his spindly nose was the biggest pair of sunglasses the girls had ever seen. And around his neck, worn as a pendant, was Carly's glitter ball!

"One two, one two!" called Jack Frost loudly into the microphone. He turned around to count the goblins in and then began to rap:

My name's Frosty and I'm the best,
I'm way cooler than all the rest!
My goblin crew is called The Gobolicious
Band,
We make the iciest sounds in all the land!

"Wow," cried Kirsty, looking surprised, "they sound amazing!"

"That's the power of my glitter ball," said Carly sadly. "And they're going to use it to show off at the school dance!"

"*Hmm,*" Rachel pondered. "I think I have an idea for how to get your glitter ball back. What does Jack Frost care about more than anything in the world?"

Kirsty thought for a moment. She frowned, and then her eyes lit up. "Himself!" she cried.

"Exactly." Rachel smiled. "Let's use that to get the glitter ball from him!"

Glitter-Ball Tricks!

The two girls and their fairy friend
bravely walked toward the big stage to
speak to Jack Frost.

"Jack Frost, can we have a word with
you, please?" Rachel called politely. Jack
Frost peered down at the girls and Carly
through his enormous sunglasses.

"What do you silly girls want?" he
asked rudely.

"We just wondered, who will do the chores in the Ice Castle when all the goblins are at school in the human world?" asked Kirsty innocently.

Jack Frost scowled. "The goblins will only be in school for a few hours each day, so they'll have plenty of time to spend on me."

Rachel stepped forward. "The thing is, after the goblins have finished the school day, there'll be after-school activities, and lots of homework. There won't be much time for anything else."

"But who will serve me yummy ice cream and massage my feet?" Jack Frost wondered.

Carly fluttered forward to address Jack Frost. "Why don't you let *me* teach the goblins? I can organize lessons at your Ice Castle. That way the goblins will have lots of time to help you. But first, I need *you* to return my glitter ball to me."

The girls exchanged a worried look. Would he be convinced?

Jack Frost narrowed his eyes. "I don't want them picking up even more bad habits! No, the goblins will be going to school here, and that's the end of it. Now, get out of my way before I turn you all into icicles!"

Jack Frost pointed his icy wand at the friends and they quickly ran down the stage.

"What do we do now?" cried Carly, her little wings drooping unhappily.

"It's time for action!" Kirsty said with a determined look on her face. "Carly, can you turn us into fairies? And would you be able to magic up one large glitter ball that's light enough for Rachel and me to carry? I've got an idea!"

"Of course!" said Carly, waving her wand. The girls felt themselves grow smaller and smaller. Shiny wings appeared on their backs and a sparkly giant glitter ball, as light as a feather, appeared in their hands!

Rachel and Kirsty flew back onto the stage, clutching the new giant glitter ball between them.

"Yoo-hoo!" they called to Jack Frost. "We just came to say we don't need your glitter ball any more because we have this amazing new one!"

"A new, giant glitter ball?" he exclaimed, his eyes widening. "Look how big it is. I want it!"

"You can have this new, super-sparkly glitter ball," said Kirsty firmly, "as long as you return the one you have to Carly. It's hers and she needs it back."

Jack Frost wasn't too sure. He looked at Carly's glitter ball around his neck and suddenly realized how small it was. "Fine," he grumbled. "This one isn't big or glittery enough anyway!" With that, he took off the glitter ball.

"Now,
Carly!" called
Rachel, and
Carly flew
onto the stage
and picked up
her magic
glitter ball. She
hugged it tight
and fluttered a
happy loop-the-
loop in the air!

"Here you go," said
Kirsty, and the two friends handed the
giant glitter ball to Jack Frost.

"Wow!" he exclaimed, holding it up to
the green lights, so that thousands of tiny
light particles glistened on the stage. The
goblins ran up to admire the new glitter

ball and Jack Frost proudly showed it off
to them.

"We did it!" cheered Rachel and
Kirsty, giving Carly a huge hug. The
three friends flew off the stage.

"Girls, you were amazing," cried Carly. "Now, I must take this back to Fairyland right away! Thank you for all your help." The little fairy quickly turned Rachel and Kirsty back into girls and then disappeared in a puff of fairy dust.

Jack Frost and his goblins headed off the stage. Jack Frost was holding the glitter ball and the goblins were jumping up and down trying to touch it.

Rachel and Kirsty shook their heads. Jack Frost seemed really happy with his new decoration.

Just then, the sound of excited voices came from the hall. The dance was about to begin!

A Magical, Musical Time

The girls quickly made their way into
the hall. Now that Carly had her glitter
ball back, everything looked amazing!
The lights flashed with all the colors
of the rainbow and the music sounded
great. The party food on the table
looked delicious, and the ceiling was
covered in lots of tiny glitter balls.

The girls were just nibbling at some of Mr. Walker's tasty cheese straws when Kirsty saw something out of the corner of her eye.

"Pssst!" It was Carly, hovering behind a heart-shaped balloon, accompanied by her friend, Jade the Disco Fairy. "Girls, I know you're having fun here, but will you come to Fairyland with us? We're having a magical party and we'd love you to join us."

"Yes, please!" chorused the girls. They knew that time in the human world would stand still while they were away, so they would still be able to come back and enjoy the school dance!

Rachel and Kirsty slipped out of the hall and stood behind a rack of coats in the hallway. They held hands as the fairies waved their wands and they were caught up in a glittering whirlwind. They were off to Fairyland!

Just a few seconds later, the girls and their fairy friends landed in the Great Hall of the Fairyland Palace. Rachel and Kirsty had been in the hall before, but they had never seen it looking so beautiful. The ceiling had been transformed into the night sky, with stars twinkling and shooting from one side to the other. The Night Fairies, who had

created the display, waved happily to the girls. Jade the Disco Fairy was joined by the other Dance Fairies, and in no time everyone was dancing to the wonderful music performed by the Music Fairies.

Queen Titania and King Oberon, the wise and kind rulers of Fairyland, came to greet the girls.

"Rachel and Kirsty, we wanted to give you a gift to say thank you for helping Carly." Queen Titania smiled. She took out two small boxes from the pocket of her robe and handed them to the girls. They gasped as they saw that each box contained a beautiful charm bracelet, complete with a glitter ball charm that sparkled under the night sky.

"Thank you so much, Your Majesties!" the girls cried, fastening the charm bracelets around their wrists.

"And now, we have a special musical surprise for you all," King Oberon called to the crowd. "Please join me in welcoming on stage Frosty and his Gobolicious Band!"

All the fairies looked surprised to see Jack Frost and his goblins as they came onto the stage, looking a little uncomfortable. As the band started to warm up, the king put an arm around each of the girls.

"You see, girls, although Jack Frost shouldn't have taken Carly's objects, he did a good thing today by returning the glitter ball. And good acts should always be rewarded. Besides, he really is a pretty good musician!" said the kind king with a twinkle in his eye.

The girls smiled and clapped as Jack Frost and his goblins started to play. In no time at all, the fairies started dancing, and Frosty's Gobolicious Band looked on top of the world!

After chatting with their friends and enjoying some delicious fizzing strawberry sundaes, it was time for Rachel and Kirsty to return to their school dance.

Carly gave the girls a huge hug and with a wave of her wand, the girls found themselves back at Tippington School.

Very soon, it was time for the award ceremony, and Kirsty was delighted that Wetherbury had won the best science experiment award for their bubble display!

"Wow, this has been such an exciting week," said Rachel as the two friends sat down in the hall, watching everyone have lots of fun.

"It's been amazing." Kirsty smiled, playing with her glitter ball charm. "I'm sad it's over but I'm sure we'll have more incredible adventures with our very special fairy friends!"

SPECIAL EDITION

Don't miss any of Rachel and Kirsty's
other fairy adventures!
Join them as they try to help

the Angel Fairy!

Read on for a special sneak peek . . .

Winter Chaos

"The Winter Fair opens in five minutes," said Rachel Walker, her eyes dancing with excitement. "Are we ready to turn on the twinkle lights?"

"Definitely!" exclaimed her best friend, Kirsty Tate.

Kirsty was staying at Rachel's house for a few days of vacation. The pair had enjoyed a wonderful week ice skating, drinking hot chocolates, and baking cookies. Time always seemed to rush by when Kirsty and Rachel were together!

Now it was Saturday afternoon and the friends were dressed in their Brownie uniforms. The girls in Rachel's troop had been working hard all morning—today was the day of the Tippington Brownies' Winter Fair! Kirsty and Rachel had volunteered to run the "winter woollies" stall, a tabletop stacked high with mittens, socks, and scarves knitted in rich, festive colors.

Rachel ran to the back of the hall. When one of the leaders gave the signal, she dimmed the main lights.

Everyone closed their eyes in the darkness and counted down together. "Three, two, one . . . go!"

Flash!

There was a thrilled gasp, then an explosion of clapping and cheering. The Brownies had transformed Tippington's plain old town hall into a magical winter wonderland! Stalls lined every wall, each one decorated with fake snow, gold balls, and shiny bows. Garlands of glittery lights twinkled from the ceiling. In the kitchen, Mrs. Walker and the other Brownie moms had been busy making hot chocolate and arranging treats, filling the air with the smell of warm cookies.

The girls had come in the day before to help deck the hall with lights, ribbons, and paper snowflakes.

Kirsty squeezed Rachel's hand and smiled. The friends shared a very special secret. From the very first day they met, the pair had been going on trips to Fairyland! They had shared some wonderful adventures with their magical friends. Both girls had made a promise to protect the fairies from Jack Frost and his grumpy goblins.

"Everybody to their positions, please," called their leader. "It's time to open the doors."

There was an excited hustle and bustle as the Brownies rushed to their stalls.

"We should raise lots of money today," said Kirsty hopefully. "Look at all these wonderful things!"

This year, the Brownies had decided to celebrate the true spirit of the holiday season. Instead of spending money on new equipment for the pack, they had chosen to buy gifts for people who weren't as lucky as they were. Giving to others was what this time of year was really all about.

"I can't wait to take a big sack of presents to Tippington Children's Hospital." Kirsty smiled. "It must be terrible to be sick at this time of year."

Rachel ran over to help another Brownie named Claire unpack the last few ornaments for her Christmas decoration stall.

"Don't forget the retirement-home visit, too!" she called back.

The Brownies had voted to spend half of the money on gifts for the children's hospital and the other half on the residents of Greenacre Retirement Home, which was just around the corner from Rachel's house.

RAINBOW magic™

SPECIAL EDITION

Which Magical Fairies Have You Met?

3 stories in each one!

- ☐ Joy the Summer Vacation Fairy
- ☐ Holly the Christmas Fairy
- ☐ Kylie the Carnival Fairy
- ☐ Stella the Star Fairy
- ☐ Shannon the Ocean Fairy
- ☐ Trixie the Halloween Fairy
- ☐ Gabriella the Snow Kingdom Fairy
- ☐ Juliet the Valentine Fairy
- ☐ Mia the Bridesmaid Fairy
- ☐ Flora the Dress-Up Fairy
- ☐ Paige the Christmas Play Fairy
- ☐ Emma the Easter Fairy
- ☐ Cara the Camp Fairy
- ☐ Destiny the Rock Star Fairy
- ☐ Belle the Birthday Fairy
- ☐ Olympia the Games Fairy
- ☐ Selena the Sleepover Fairy
- ☐ Cheryl the Christmas Tree Fairy
- ☐ Florence the Friendship Fairy
- ☐ Lindsay the Luck Fairy
- ☐ Brianna the Tooth Fairy
- ☐ Autumn the Falling Leaves Fairy
- ☐ Keira the Movie Star Fairy
- ☐ Addison the April Fool's Day Fairy
- ☐ Bailey the Babysitter Fairy
- ☐ Natalie the Christmas Stocking Fairy
- ☐ Lila and Myla the Twins Fairies
- ☐ Chelsea the Congratulations Fairy

Find all of your favorite fairy friends at
scholastic.com/rainbowmagic

HIT entertainment

RMSPECIAL15